Meatheads Say the Realest Things

A Satirical (Short) Novel of the Last Bro

Colin Fleming

TP

TAILWINDS PRESS

Tailwinds Press
P.O. Box 2283, Radio City Station
New York, NY 10101-2283
www.tailwindspress.com

Published in the United States of America
ISBN: 978-1-7356016-2-5
1ˢᵗ ed. 2020

Meatheads Say the Realest Things

CHAPTER 1
"Phone Call"

"Bro," a meathead said to his mom whom he had phoned. "I need to talk to you. For real this time."

She hesitated, then asked him if it was not for pretend.

This was confusing.

"What are you talking about, ma? It's really me and this is really you. We aren't pretend."

He was worried that maybe he was a twin of himself in a different dimension. Like the ghost dimension.

"Stop it, ma. For real."

The meathead's name was Chad. It was a

good meathead name. Lots of meatheads went by it.

Chad liked his name because in grammar school he was Rad Chad. At football with his teammates he was known as Chad the Gonad. Some science doofus in eighth grade called him Chad the Impaler because he hooked up with lots of girls but he didn't understand that reference. Maybe it came from a book. Books could be problematic. Also, frightening. In high school he'd kiss the cover of a book when he was alone to start off his relationship with it right, but the only person Chad might have told about this was an imaginary friend.

"Come on, ma. I didn't do nothing. Is this because I word-blasted you last time?"

He liked his new term. It sounded smart. But it made him think of the video he had watched the evening before to cheer himself up.

A man called the Blaster stood over a woman he had been romancing. His arms were spread open like he'd just finished hugging a super-sized apple. The woman was wiping her face. Then the Blaster said, approvingly, "Now that's richly coated." He was very pleased with his work. Chad thought of caramel-covered apples. They were good. He should eat more of them. But wait.

Chad shuddered. The pain was too new. At least he was hungry. A start, anyway.

His mother pointed out that he had told her not to call him again until she was terminal.

"I called you, ma."

He was informed that was not the point.

Chad understood. Now was the time when it was important to become very serious.

"Look, bro, I meant when you hit terminal

velocity. Like when you really got it going on. When you are your best self. Love, live, laugh. You know me, ma."

But he still didn't like the question his mother had asked him.

"Yeah, ma, Karen dumped the C-Note"— the totes cool name he invented for life's keeping it real moments—"and we were doing so good. So good, ma."

Chad thought it would be best to show how hurt he was by revealing more of himself than usual. He imagined his neck had been twisted into a knot. He winced. And also thought of pretzels. A pretzel could hit the spot. He should eat more pretzels. He would. They would not stop him.

"Ma, we were tight. I plugged all of her holes. But I didn't plug her mouth. I kept her mouth free."

Chad's mother found this at best worrisome, and at second best felonious. The astrophysicist that she told Chad was his father taught her all she needed to know about the old adage that a scientist like Karen and a Chad might not be the best mix.

"Because that was the one hole that bad stuff came out, ma. The hurting stuff. Like, 'Chad, we can't do this anymore. And I know that you're going to call me baby girl, but we are past that.' You see, ma? Past even that. O my baby girl. If I could have just plugged that hole too . . ."

He sniffled.

"She hole-blasted me, ma. Blasted a hole . . ."

Was he going to say it?

" . . . in my heart."

He did.

Then he thought for a moment.

"Ma, I shouldn't have word-blasted you. You know when my feelz kick in, I am a rhino. Hehaw, huff huff hut."

His mother asked him if he had watched the Patriots game the other day, but Chad said, "Not now, ma, it's time to heal. Some day my rhino horn may grow again. Good talking to you, ma. Stay terminal."

Click.

Chad thought about watching the Blaster's video again—actually, he had a full channel of similarly themed videos—but he decided he would call his friend Ungar instead. Or maybe do both at the same time. They were pretty comfortable with each other. More or less.

"Yo, Ung Man, it's Impaler."

"'Sup, ma."

"Why you calling me ma, bro?"

"Why are you bothering my ass at noon on a Saturday, ma? When I is about to get suuuuuccckked."

Ungar was crazy.

"Look, Ung Man, I have to tell you something. It's about me and my baby girl, Karen. She blasted me, bro. She hole-blasted me. Blasted a hole . . . " He paused, sniffed, imagined he was in Metallica, then continued. " . . . made a hole. In my heart."

"You need to fill that hole," Ungar replied.

Chad felt his breaths become shorter and his heart beat faster as he waited for Ungar to continue. "Pumpedalicous," he softly said to himself in his brain.

"And you know what you need to fill it with?"

He had the right answer waiting for this one. "My dick."

"Yeah, bro. Fill that shit. You a warrior, my

rhino. Huff huff hut."

"Later, Ungar. Cheers." "Cheers" was another word you could use to sound smart.

"Later, Impaler."

Ungar rolled onto his back, and waited.

"Who was that?" Karen asked.

"That was my boy."

CHAPTER 2
"The Symphony"

"Bronado, this shit be fancy, yo," a meathead named Chad said to his girlfriend.

This is not necessarily the Chad we have already encountered, but it is not necessarily not him either. We are trusting your judgment in these matters. But you should probably think of him as a representative of Meathead Nation. Meatheads are good sports, so their wrath need not be feared. We can all learn from the meathead. Until we can learn no more.

Chad and Clarice had just taken their seats in the balcony at the symphony.

"Babe, my phone is locked and loaded on

that Patriots game. So, like, if they be scoring, I'm gonna be shouting out the glad tidings. Brady roolz, mofos!"

He had recently learned the phrase "glad tidings." It was Christmas and his therapist had advised him to be more in touch with the season this year. "Time and tide wait for no man," the therapist had said. "Get festive." Which Chad heard as, "Balls deep."

"Tide rolls in, tide rolls out, tide gets you super wet ta ha ha ha ha ta ha. Don't you feel grown up when you're here? Ta ha ta ha."

Clarice couldn't help but notice that some men like Chad had a tendency to insert a "t" into their laughter, which already sounded like barrels rolling.

Her therapist had said she should extend her parameters. "Not everyone has to be a surgeon. Be ecumenical in your search. People have a way of surprising us." Clarice thought maybe it was time for a new therapist.

"You diggin' what the 'Dolph is up to?" Chad inquired, rubbing the undercarriage of the famous red-nosed Christmas reindeer who covered his entire sweater front. "The 'Dolph is like, 'You know why it's red.' Nothing makes itself red on its own. Not even kisses."

And he winked.

"Deal sealer," he inwardly opined.

Chad had never seen Handel's *Messiah*. A laser show seemed a possibility.

"So like Handle Mariah was this chick who did Spotify before anyone did Spotify. FACKS. Tres coolio."

Normally Chad would not do research before a date, but he had decided he was going to be in love soon. And speaking Spanish at Christmastime was a good way to show that you were welcoming of all cultures. His friend Trey had said so at the bar.

"You be roping in the cattle from all the lady nations," Trey concluded. "Gotta bust a bronc to get rode, yo."

Chad pondered this. Then, theorized.

"It's like putting the star on the top of the tree, bro. You fall forwards, you eat the needles. Fall backwards, the needles eat you. But you don't want to eat like that, my brother, you know what I mean? Ta ha ha ha. Ta ha ha ta ha."

Trey had no clue.

"Babe, why are those people below us blue?" Chad asked, pointing to the crowd on the main floor.

Clarice was starting to think she had made a dire mistake.

"They're just older."

"How old?"

"I don't know. Like seventies?"

"So north of sixty-nine. Ta ha ha ta ha ha ta ha. Yeah. You get it. You're picking up what I'm putting down. Swizzle stick on the ground. Pick it up. Pop it in the mouth. Now lick, and spit, spit, and lick. Mouth pop. Mouth pop, mouth pop, you feel it, you feel it, you need it, that's right that's right, mouth pop."

He sang these words to the tune of the *Hallelujah* chorus. Research had paid off.

As he extended his balled-up hand for a fist bump, a young boy in a suit sitting between Chad and Clarice smacked his forehead. The couple had gotten their tickets last minute.

"What's up, little 'Dolph?" Chad asked. The boy looked very smart and he made Chad a little nervous.

"Why are you making sixty-nine jokes?

Stand down. Robespierre. And apologize. Sir."

"What?"

Clarice piped in. "It's okay. Thank you."

But Chad did not stand for blown-up spots.

"No, screw this. What's up with you, bro? Why are you blowing up my spot?" He puffed out his cheeks.

This meant business. His underbite was reserved for orgasms. But when forced—

The boy started to shake. As Chad reasoned—inwardly (he was getting better at his inside voice)—this wasn't a dog you could slap.

"What would Yoda do?" he asked, also inwardly.

Two for two.

"Come on, bro, don't cry. Look, Rudolph."

He began to rub Rudolph's undercarriage portion.

"Feels good. All warm inside. Wait, what's

this? My phone?"

The orchestra was almost done tuning up. The conductor waited in the wings.

"Update to the Patriots game?" Chad pantomimed checking a website on his phone. "Patriots up 56-7? They be whaling. Don't cry little man. Mini bro. Bro Junior. My little BJ."

The lights went down. Tears were on the boy's cheeks.

"There there," said Clarice, taking his hand.

Maybe she would adopt after all.

"Oh fuck me," Chad said as he pulled out his phone six bars into the orchestra's opening movement.

The blue-colored people from down below looked up at him in the balcony.

"Didn't charge it, bros," he mouthed sadly, moving the phone from left to right and back again by the side of his face. "No me chargo."

CHAPTER 3
"The Therapist"

"Chad, bro," a meathead named Chad said to himself as he looked at himself in the mirror, wrapped in his New England Patriots towel. "I know you got this, bro, and I got you."

Chad liked post-shower Chad.

He used his left hand to cup his right bicep. He inhaled deeply.

"Lilac-scented Chad is still bad Chad, amirite ladies? Ta ha ha. Ta ha ta ha."

The mirror was even more generous than usual.

Then it was time to get serious. Like a championship team returning to the field after a timeout with its season on the line.

"Hug it out," he said to his hand and his bicep, which were still interlocked. "That's it, boys. Chad group hug. Bring it in."

He became a little weepy as he kissed his bicep and got a little of his hand in his mouth, too.

"Is this something you do every time before you come to see me?" Chad's therapist asked. "Or was it just today?"

Chad was confused that he could be asked such a thing.

"I always come hard when I come for you, bro. This ain't easy for me, doc. You realize I'm a warrior, right? People who see me on the street be like, 'Where is your spear my dog' and I say, 'That shit is in the shop because assholes don't sharpen themselves ta ha ta ha and a warrior spear is a business spear, does the dirty work nice spears don't do. So if they're knowing my warrior brain gets a tune-up, I is cooked as they say—you can't show weakness, bro. I was so down the other day, because, you know, like, life, he can be a prick, right, speaking of assholes, so I'm like, 'Screw yourself, life, Chad is getting up because Chad is hard,' and like a man I took that whole bottle of pills you gave me. Didn't do nothing."

The therapist informed Chad that they were not to be taken all at once.

"I know you've said that, doc, but I gave myself a second opinion ta ha ha. I used to watch Popeye—so this is that childhood stuff you dig—and when he was down he always ate that whole can, bro, he wasn't like, 'Give me a leaf,' nah, he was like, watch, bitches, watch what you did now, here comes a bad mofo, here he comes. BEAST UNLEASHED.

RECKONING. And my bad mofo self, he ain't coming for me any more, doc. It's like warrior Chad gets locked in a closet, and he wants to get out. So I'm like, 'Chad, I got you, have all the pills and get out of the closet.'"

"Hmmmm," said the therapist, making a note in his notebook, before proceeding to ask questions that Chad did not care for.

If he was seeing anyone.

("Me and this girl were going to have a threesome with this other girl, but the storage room was locked.")

If he had threatened his mother.

("If by threatened you mean blew her ass up with a truth bomb, yeah. But I need to see her Tuesday 'cause something is wrong with the data on my phone.")

If there was more to the weekend than beer and football.

("I don't know, bro," Chad said, looking behind the doctor at the wall. "Is there more than diplomas in frames if you're a doc? 'Cause I could be you. 'Tell me what's wrong. Are you sad that you're old? Don't take all the pills at once.' I checked you, bro. We even now.")

If his sister's husband was going to sue over the broken nose.

"Look, my brother, I told you what he said. He called me fat. It has to stop somewhere. And it stopped here."

Chad held up his fist.

"But that's not what happened, is it?" asked the therapist.

"Nah, bro. He fell on the ice. But mostly because he knew I was coming."

The therapist asked Chad if he was bothered that he didn't talk to his sister as much as he used to now that she was married.

Chad reached for the Oscar the Grouch stuffed animal that was part of his therapy. It sat on the chair beside him, until a certain moment.

"So, like, you know how you do prescriptions and I do prescriptions and I got my brother Oscar here to reinforce right from wrong?"

("Reinforce," Chad found, was a good word to use when in doubt.)

"Because I ain't going down that Oscar hole. Shit got dark for him, man. In that trash can. Life's like a can, my brother. Then the world puts the lid on you, and some dude named Sully the garbage man carries you around. Fuck that shit."

Chad gave his hips one single resolute forward pump in his chair.

The therapist pointed to his watch.

"We have come to the end of our time."

Chad was not in a position to be stopped.

"I ain't in a position to be stopped, doc. You know how it is. Look at Oscar's giant eyebrow. Doesn't even groom himself, bro. Look at mine. Two. Right? I manage that shit. Like at the gym, when I'm doing my Chads—that's what I call my deluxe workout—and I'm looking in the mirror, it's like shit, boy, nice brows, nice separation, and yeah, I'll say it, nice package. Ha ha ta ha ha ta."

The doctor asked if he wanted a tissue. The certain moment had come.

"I miss my sis, bro. Like who am I supposed to be texting now? You know what they say, Ali G, marriage makes hoes."

He flung Oscar the Grouch towards the corner he normally flung him at.

"Shit, you can hear his eyes hit the wall. Sorry, green bro. I'll be right back, man."

Chad left the room. He returned carrying a chair from the waiting room.

"She'll take it."

The doctor asked who would take what. Chad left again, leaving the door open. This time his sister walked in, with Chad behind her.

"If she can be fixed, doc, I give her to you. This is what I like to call the Real Room, bro," Chad said to his sister. "It gets so real ain't nothing real anymore in the world outside. Trust the process."

He had told his bicep the same thing before he kissed it and tasted a bit of his hand earlier.

"What can I do for you?" the doctor asked Chad's sister, after Chad had left the room again, manfully holding back his tears of presumed sagacity.

"Nothing. Sorry. I'm my brother's ride. He'll be in next week."

CHAPTER 4
"Tidal Pool"

"Bro, bro," and "'Sup, bro," a meathead named Chad and a meathead named Ungar said to each other early one morning when getting on a school bus.

The double honorific was one Chad rarely used. We may say many things about the meathead. But the meathead can have true value. He can remind us that at any time in this life, someone may surprise us. And that is not a bad thing.

Ungar asked Chad if he was ready to do this shit. They were chaperoning a school field trip for Ungar's daughter's class to the salt marshes of Ipswich. Ungar volunteered Chad to help so he would have someone to hang out with when he got bored.

"I was on the 'Ball last night, if you know what I mean, C-Note."

This remark confused Chad. He thought maybe Ungar was choosing to reveal something at a strange time.

"I am here for you, Bro bro."

"The Fireball. Glug glug glug ta ha ha ta ha."

What a relief.

Chad was drinking a large coffee from Dunkin' Donuts with eighteen packets of Splenda in it.

Ungar had once said, "You know, bro, I used to think that dude was named Duncan—D-U-N-C-A-N—like that king bro in Shakespeare, and he had a coffee biz, and it was like, 'Cray! Diversified assets!'"

Chad thought this was insanely intelligent.

The sea smelled nice. The sand was crunchy. Chad liked sand crunch, but he didn't like sand in his sandwiches when he went to the beach. Sandwiches were sacred.

"I am out, bro," Ungar said, after the bus had arrived at the nature center and Ungar ran off with his daughter, Emma.

She was popular. A girl on the bus had brought a lanyard she made for Emma and gave it to her and when Emma put it around her neck, the girl smiled so hard back at Emma that Chad smiled also and said, "Circle of life," and Ungar told him not to be gay.

"Hello," said a girl who came up not much beyond Chad's thigh, so that he had nearly walked into her, as he wondered what the hell he was supposed to do now that he was alone and kids and teachers and the Ung Man were gone.

"I'm Dolores," she said. "I always get left behind."

"That blows, Little Miss. People be like, 'Yo yo yo, let's do yo yo yo,' and sometimes there aren't enough yo's, you know?"

"Yo."

Chad liked this girl.

After he told her his name and she agreed to call him C-Note, they walked in a different direction from the one in which everyone else had gone.

"Yo, my pops brought me here when I was a mini-Note," Chad said. "I got you. We'll have fun."

Dolores asked Chad if he had any kids. He said no and maybe he never would. And if he had a wife. He said that someday he would have a baby girl, which was confusing, but she thought she knew what he probably meant.

The sand became even crunchier.

"Don't you think it's like granola?" Dolores asked, and Chad liked her question, because he liked granola a lot.

"The gran-gran is good for you, br—"

He stopped himself.

"You were going to call me bro, weren't you? Why do you call people bro?"

Chad pretended to think for a moment, but he didn't really have to.

"I call people I like bro." Then he paused, because he did have to. "Or people I want to like me."

"Word, bro."

"You get it. Girl bro."

They had arrived at the spot Chad was looking for. It was a tidal pool and Chad loved to smell tidal pools. He ranked his favorite smells.

"People be like tearing it down, but the gym is the smell of self-improvement."

Dolores was rapt. So Chad continued.

"Then gasoline is pretty good. Cut grass. And this tidal pool, practice child."

"You're funny."

"Ta ha ha ha ta ha."

They leaned over the edge of the pool. There were urchins, rock crabs, razor clams. Chad pulled out a starfish and then the Swiss Army knife he always kept on him, just in case. A lot of people want to take a big man down, his pops had once told him.

"Oh no!" Dolores shrieked.

"Nah, it's cool," Chad said, as he sawed off the arm of a starfish he had pulled out of the pool and set down on the rock they were crouched upon.

"This bro here, he don't even feel this. And he's like, 'C-Note, you gotta understand, I'm outsmarting you, with your knife, super powerful that you are, because I don't feel this and the parts you cut from me just grow back.' Ah, starfish bro."

Chad stifled a manful sigh, which was sometimes a prelude to a manful sob.

"And this right here is the circle of life," he continued.

He plucked a hermit crab from the pool and placed it upon the starfish's severed limb. The crab began to eat.

"Look at that dude nosh. Ta ha. Today has been a good day."

Dolores had taken the knife and stuck it through the back of a horseshoe crab.

"Bro, how come it's just sinking and not fixing itself?" she asked.

Chad said that that particular animal should maybe be their secret animal and she probably shouldn't tell anyone and to only slice apart starfish. He could not believe how mature he sounded. It was true, perhaps: kids really brought it out of you.

They rode back on the bus together, and in the school parking lot Chad met Dolores' mother.

"Damn, practice kid, your mom is smoking hot," he said, before Dolores introduced them and raced off to their car.

"I was just out with, like, girl bro, just us. Ta ha. Kids. Kids, right? Sometimes they're not . . . "

"Nice?"

"Yeah. Nice. But sometimes they are."

Dolores' mom smiled. Maybe this was the one. A couple eighteen Splenda-laced coffees seemed a good place to start.

"You know, I used to think Dunkin' Donuts was spelled D-U . . . shit . . . N-K . . . wait . . . A-N, like that king from Shakespeare and it was like poet dude had a side gig. Ta ha ha. Ta ha ha ta."

CHAPTER 5
"Sleep Study"

"But bro," a meathead named Chad said to a nurse who had told him he had to keep his shorts on. He was hooked up to many machines and not in the mood for further confinement.

Does the universe send out signals that we may be the unwitting recipients of? Chad sometimes thought this was indeed the case. He called it a "universe poke."

We sometimes think it, too, and that is why we should gently remind you that this Chad is not necessarily the Chad of past adventures, nor was the last Chad the Chad before that.

Oh, sure, we could tell you about a meat-head named Darren, and a meathead named Rocco, probably less about a meathead named Clive—though you never know—but let us just stick with Chad, even if each Chad does not necessarily stick with the other Chads.

"Shit be real, bro."

Yes. He is correct there. It be.

Chad had many night terrors and he rode the T a lot.

(Wait, our bad—all of these Chads lived in Boston or passed through there at some point. "Meta, bro." No. Stop it. We are not going down that road. Authorial-input Chad, you pipe down, and let us get back to the business of the other Chads.)

As we were saying.

One day on the T, which is the subway, as Chad headed to Revere Beach for some sun and skin—for Chad had bitchin' sunglasses that were good for ogling the la-la-ladies—he saw an ad for a sleep study for people with nightmares and night terrors. They were different from each other, but Chad often had both.

"Fifty bucks to go to bed? And the bed has rails so you can't even fall out? Hmmm." Chad was stoked.

Once Chad produced a "hmmm" it was nearly certain that he was going to do whatever it was that first made him make the hmmm sound.

But he did not like to be restricted when he slept.

"Look. What I am talking about, bro, is called the art of compromise," he said to the nurse. Her name was Carol. She was smoking hot, but this was not about that. This was about wisdom and precautionary measures.

"Normally, and I don't mean this to get you going, like, for realz, I get that you're working and can't hook up or anything at work and probably all you can do is touch yourself in a closet. We cool. I respect you. But normally I have to be clothes-free Chad to sleep. Or we are going into the Terror Dome. So what I'm saying is, I'll keep my top on, for you, because that helps you keep your job, but down below, underneath the covers, where it is intense, especially at night, when anything can happen, I need to be free. Free me, fellow C-Dawg."

He scooched his hips into the air. Carol would have something to tell her fellow nurses about later, and for a long time after, but if the God of Reality were to tap Chad on the shoulder and inform Chad that Carol would be talking about him deep into her future, he likely would have guessed for another reason.

Like his quads. Conceivably the outline of juicy parts. "These things happen, God of Reality, bro," Chad might have said, and the God of Reality may well have gotten drunk after on account of he or she being sad.

Chad was set on fire a lot in his dreams. The worst part about it was he was almost always the one who lit the flames. Sometimes he set his studio apartment on fire. Other times he blew up his own car. At the Fourth of July, in his Dream Land, there were bonfires on beaches that he leapt into. He sure as shit ended up in hell a lot, and that was nothing but fire. There had been a pre-study interview.

"Doc, in the hell one, Dream Chad—you can just use DC on the form, like the comic books"—for Chad intuited that doctors were probably readers and they had a lot of down time at work—"goes to take a break from working in the fire fields growing Satan's herbs, because that's what you do for work there, and he tries to take a shower but when he turns on the faucet all of these flames come out. He gets flame-blasted right in the face. Then when he tries to clean his darkest places, you know what I mean as a medical man, you can imagine how real that shit gets. Bad real. Not magical feeling real. You extra know what I mean by that. Ta ha ha ha ta."

Then he thought of a joke.

"Shower head. Get it? Ta ha."

As Chad lay in bed, hooked up to machines, with his top and his bottoms on, he began to think that maybe Dream Chad wasn't such an ally after all.

There was the possibility that he was an inversion of everything decent about Real Chad. Chad did not quite put it this way.

"I think Dream Chad might be an ass backwards little Beta Boy."

There. He had said it. Or thought it. He couldn't remember which. So he then said it, just so that it was on the universe's official record.

Chad figured that God probably recorded everything. No sense not making it official, just in case someone accused him later of thinking something else.

"No dealio, God," Chad also said, before mouthing that he was sorry and had not intended to transgress, which was a word Chad actually knew and used a lot, given that he knew that one.

"Who wouldn't, right?" as he concluded.

But a Beta Boy! He might as well have called Dream Chad . . . Pontius Pilate. Wait. He didn't know that one. Darth Vader. Wait.

Vader was an ass kicker.

Well, anyhow, someone really bad who was a man but not a real man and someone who showed weakness rather than being strong enough to hide it and pretend everything was fine.

As he became more and more tired, Chad thought harder and harder about his new theory that the clothes he wore to bed in the real world followed him into his dream and made it easier for him to be set on fire.

In sixth grade a teacher had told Chad's class that a lot of women in Victorian times caught on fire because of the clothes they wore, which led Chad to turn to Anna Davis next to him—"Smoking hot, natch"—(naturally)—and say, "'Sup? I know how that can be fixed ta ha ha ha ta ha."

Detention sucked.

But so did trying to kill Dream Chad, which is what regular Chad ("ain't nothing regular about me, bro") had set out to do.

It was like a sleep study miracle. Real Chad had somehow, via the divine grace of said miracle, made it through the blockade that separates Reality from Dream.

He stood naked—"Result!" as Real Chad put it when he emerged into Dream World—in front of Dream Chad.

They were in hell, working Satan's fields.

"Why are you blowing up my dream spot?" RC asked.

"How dare you level such a charge at me," DC replied.

"Whoa, bro."

"You didn't know we were this smart, did you?"

"I sensed it, my brother. Dream brother."

They hugged it out.

"I will return to the surface world now," naked Chad concluded. "Keep fighting the Chad-erific fight in these fields of Satan."

And with that, he departed, and awoke.

"Jackass," thought Dream Chad, who then said it aloud as he picked up his hoe again, just to make sure his thoughts made it into hell's official record.

"Because everything is recorded, you know."

CHAPTER 6
"Jazz Bar"

"Blow, bro!" a meathead named Chad yelled out 'round midnight.

This was a new experience for Chad. He was at a jazz bar with his cousin Tony C. and Tony C.'s two dates.

Tony C. studied trombone at Berklee, which was a music college, and wore a pork pie hat. Even Chad had to admit, it was harder to be cooler than Tony C. And he was big. It seemed like Tony C. had it all.

New experiences meant new phrases, which Chad liked, being a man of the world and a neologism buff.

Ha.

Well.

In his way.

When he was a boy and his dad took him to his first baseball game at Fenway, his dad said, "Now if you are a batter you want to get steaks."

This sounded magical. Already at seven, Chad was a big fan of steaks, though he did not know how large they would loom in his legacy in terms of making him strong.

And from strength came smartness. Not enough people knew that as well as Chad, which made him sad.

"Run Batted In," his dad said. "RBI. Sound it out."

Quite a large number of individuals were going to say that phrase to Chad, but he did not know it yet. So he just stared at his father.

"R-B-I. Ribeye! Steaks!"

It would take a long time for Chad to grasp his father's wisdom, but that was part of becoming a man.

So he had six Fenway Franks instead.

Chad liked the jazz bar because everyone yelled the word "blow," but it was classy.

Sure, it took him a while to get the hang of it, and the first few times he yelled the word he couldn't help himself from putting a "baby girl" at the end, but that was life, even at a jazz bar.

"Yo, TC, bro," Chad piped up, when the two women went to the bathroom together, "Why do you need two dates at once?"

Tony C. thought his cousin Chad was somewhat remedial.

"What's up with you, Sped? Girl, back-up girl. Duh. Plan A, Plan B. And sometimes things work out so that you end up with Plan

Double A. AA. Right?"

Chad wasn't sure. He looked at his plastic jack and Coke cup. He had gone through seven of them to try and relax. He had heard about AA.

"What are you saying, bro?"

Normally when he was supposed to visit his mother because something was wrong with his phone plan and there were lots of cars outside he just drove by because he did not want to be caught in one of those interventions. On TV they always seemed like a giant ass buzz kill.

"Can't I just have the Ella one?" Chad asked.

The women had returned and had been sitting down again for a couple minutes.

"Did you seriously just ask if you could have me?" Ella said, drinking the rest of Chad's drink.

"Don't do me hard, baby girl."

"I'm not going to do you at all."

This was not the kind of banter that Chad enjoyed.

It was way better to argue that Tom Brady was like Aquaman with powers on the land as good as his powers in the sea so it was like Aquaman was the king of all and Tom Brady was too and that was why he could play in the NBA if he wanted.

"Land, and sea. You get it," Chad would say to his fellows, who also had on Brady jerseys, or sometimes Gronkowski or Edelman ones, which were welcome to lesser degrees. Hot takes like that usually made people think hard. Chad called them Brain Poppers.

He was pretty sure he had not popped Ella's brain. Not in the way he wanted to, anyway.

He turned his attention to the music. A new

saxophone player had joined the band on stage and it was his turn to solo. He soloed for five straight minutes and Chad did not say a word, he did not even yell "blow." This was better than anything he had ever heard.

Ella had come around the table and sat down next to him. The other woman was named Danielle. Her tongue was in Tony C.'s mouth and his pork pie hat atop her head.

"I know you didn't mean it that way, I was just busting your balls," Ella said.

Now, ball busting, that was something Chad could get on board with.

"That solo blew," he said. Then he caught himself, like Tom Brady sometimes caught himself when he wanted to throw the ball down the field to Edelman, but a defensive back was about to jump the route and so Tom Brady threw the ball to Rob Gronkowski instead and that was also glorious. "Yo, I didn't mean it like that."

"I know how you meant it," Ella said. She wrote on jazz for a magazine for her work and she made Chad a little nervous, so he said, "I could write on football for my work if, like, the tickets were free. Or be a GM but that takes longer and you have to know someone."

Ella asked Chad if he wanted to play a game, which Chad understood to be her way of continuing the football theme because she was into it now, so he said, "Fuck yeah, but I'll probably destroy you so don't take it personal," and she said, no, a different game.

"I'm going to ask you what your favorite album is by my favorite jazz musician and if I think it's a good choice you can come back to my place and we will ditch your loser cousin and my drunk friend."

It was imponderable to Chad that someone could talk about Tony C. this way. Maybe there was more to the world than what he mostly knew about it.

"Nah," Chad thought, successful in not saying this word aloud, which spoke to his prodigious stores of mental discipline. Mental discipline was what allowed Chad to do so many more reps than other people who would literally be shitting themselves. The word "literally" echoed often in Chad's brain. He thought it meant "extra really" but was not totes sure.

"Like, literally?"

"No, figuratively. Yes, of course literally."

Whew.

Chad didn't know what had happened there exactly, but it seemed to have gone okay.

"My favorite jazz musician is Horace Silver,"

Ella said.

Chad liked games. He was always good at the word association game with his therapist.

"Mother," the therapist said.

"Cow," responded Chad. "No, wait—chocolate ice cream. Final answer ta ha ha ha ta ha."

Chad leaned in closer to Ella. His shirt puffed out and now he could behold his own nipples as he looked down his shirt at his chest, but this time it wasn't his own nipples he was interested in.

"Look at my chains, baby girl. You say Silver, and the C-Dawg says Gold. Yeah. Unh huh. Unh huh. Unh huh."

"Close enough. Let's go."

And so they did.

"Thrice, bro."

Chad did not actually say thrice.

We added that in.

But they had sex three times. Then they never talked again.

Chad did download a Horace Silver album, though, and he found it helped him to lift at the gym. Not win-win. But win-lose-win.

Chapter 7
"Fishing Trip"

"Brochachos," said a meathead named Chad, immediately regretting the word he had used for his rallying cry speech, considering that it sounded like nachos and here he was with his crew, six people in a small boat without power deep at sea.

Chad and some bros had decided to go drunk-fishing off of Cape Cod. As Chad liked to say, fish tasted better when you were drunk. Everything did. Except subs, because they always tasted the same, which was great, and not possible of being improved upon.

Chad's friend Ungar was the most drunk

and had unloosened the motor and knocked it into the sea.

"Real men row their bitches ashore, so let's row this bitch, bitches," Ungar had instructed.

Chad was game. He once got really drunk at the Head of the Charles regatta and throwing up on his shoes did not stop him from asking out a Harvard girl who said the word "patriarchy" to Chad which made him nervous but also feel smart to be in on such an intellectual conversation.

But their sea situation wasn't so rosy.

"Yo, Ung Man," Chad said. "Where these oars be at? Did you fold them up or some shit?"

M. Poirot and Sherlock Holmes would not have had to put noggins together to deduce that there were no oars.

The Coast Guard was called, but the Coast Guard did not immediately come.

As Chad looked at his brothers, shirts off in the sun, drinking more beers, he understood that they had bravely come to accept their fate, and one by one, calm even at the end, the others went to sleep.

He got it.

"But I don't need to accept it," Chad rallied.

Then he thought of Tom Brady.

Once upon a time, Tom Brady was behind 28-3 in the Super Bowl, and there were like only six minutes left.

Chad accepted that Tom Brady was never going to die because the great ones never really do, he liked to say, they live forever, but even Brady was probably going to die in terms of losing that game which as Chad knew was maybe even worse than dying if you were one of the great ones as Tom Brady was and the guys on this boat kind of were as well, especially Ungar, despite his fucking up today.

Even Brady fumbled.

Even Brady fumbled.

"Think about it, Chad bro," Chad thought to himself.

Or maybe Ungar was just so wise this was his way of teaching the boys a lesson.

Yes. Maybe that was it.

It probably was it.

Somebody had to go first. So Chad grabbed an empty can of Natural Light, pulled down his tight shorts, and urinated into the can.

"Bros," he said, trying to wake everyone up, "we have to hydrate."

Hydration was a code of honor and life with Chad. Once he had a date who took him to Forest Hills Cemetery because she was a poet and she thought it was beautiful there.

Chad just saw a lot of flowers and trees and

birds, but he wasn't going to blow up her spot and say that this place sucked ass.

They came to a grave and Chad's date Kristin did the math of the dates on the stone as Chad tried to and she said, "Wow, he died when he was only twenty-seven."

But Chad understood. He understood deeply.

"Hydration, baby girl. You need to hydrate. Like, you literally need to hydrate. Super literally."

The poetess knew that she would never see Chad again, but there was a good chance he would turn up in a poem of hers, if she was doing one that protested against sports and how they add nothing to society.

Yes, that would work.

"Did you just drink your piss?" Chad's friend Trey asked, as a fish hopped on his line.

Chad did not like to be remonstrated. He was trying to lead by example.

"Gather 'round, bros," he said, pretending he was Coach Belichick.

Actually, Belichick had a boat and liked to fish. Chad had seen a YouTube video about it. It was saved to his favorites. Maybe Belichick would pass by and pick them up. That would solve their problems, and could be so much more. Maybe even lead to a job as strength coach.

"No, don't be greedy, C-Note," Chad thought to himself, with his bros gathered 'round. "Assistant strength coach. Work your way up, big man."

"We don't need to drink the piss," Ungar chimed in. "We just need to literally catch a shit ton of fish and drink their blood. It has protein in it."

Protein was like the magical word for Chad and his friends. From protein came strength. From strength came hope. And the sun.

But lo, what was this? There was the sound of another boat advancing across the becalmed ocean blue. Could it be—

Would it be—

Might it divinely be—

"Coach B?" Chad tremulously uttered, and his crewmates on this journey of courage and endurance asked him, all at once, what he meant, tell them now, goddammit.

It was the Coast Guard.

"How often are we going to have to pick you guys up?" one of the officers said.

Ungar was the spokesperson.

"You know how it is, Coastie bros. It's between us and the sea."

Trey winked at Chad as he tossed a line to

the Coast Guard officer.

"I respect you for what you did for us. I didn't want to drink fish blood."

It was a confusing exchange for Chad, but they were safe.

So safe.

CHAPTER 8
"Spirit Visit"

"Is this really happening, bro?" a meathead named Chad asked a shadow that he was pretty sure was his father's ghost.

This occurred sometimes when he ate mushrooms and Twix.

"You got to fuel up, self-brother," Chad would say to himself. "Mind and body. Shaman juju. Hooya hooya."

Such was the manner in which Chad cleaned his mind on occasion. He gave it a prostate exam. To Chad this meant that he was very thorough and did whatever it took.

And so he would chant in his apartment as

he unwrapped the Twix bars and swallowed the mushrooms.

"Hooya hooya hooya hooya."

Chad had long been in touch with portions of the spirit world.

In high school there was a popular girl named Kate. Chad's teammates on the football team said she had albino nipples. Chad did not know what this meant.

"They're white, my dawg," a fellow beefy offensive lineman had said. "Like Casper the very friendly ghost, amirite? You need to see them Casper titties."

Then everyone else in the locker room laughed like they were elephants with car horns built into their snouts.

Chad asked out Kate. She was dubious of his intentions and turned him down twelve times.

"But I wore her down, bro," Chad said to his fellow O-line mate. "I pancake blocked her resistance," he concluded. Holy shit that had sounded smart.

After a movie Chad drove Kate to a place that was kind of in the woods but only about a hundred yards from the road called The Cliffs. Kids jumped off of these cliffs into a pond when it was daylight. The dashboard light was on and Kate unbuttoned her shirt. She was not wearing a bra.

"Is this what it was so important for you to see?" she asked Chad.

Chad looked down, then he looked up. Then he looked down again, and up again.

He wasn't trying to be noble. It just came out that way.

"No, Kate, dude. I came out to see your face. To me, your face is your chest. That is what I want to see. The face, Kate. The face."

That was Chad's first blowjob, and he wasn't even trying for it. He meant what he said about the face-breasts. They dated for three weeks. Then they were just friends. Chad had liked it better after they dated.

"Why do you remember pussy stories like that in your mind when I visit?" Chad's dad's ghost asked.

Chad was in his tub lying on his back. The water felt nice.

"I know you don't mean that, ghost bro dad. I thought you'd be proud."

Chad's ghost dad expostulated that he had never been told about this Kate girl. He asked what she was up to now.

"Well," Chad replied, "I check on that pretty much literally every day on Facebook to see if she gets divorced. They seem to be going strong, though, so that blows. Different kind of blow. Ta ha ha ha ta ha."

He raised his wet right hand, which had been resting on his stomach, for a ghost high five, but felt a little ashamed when his father did not reciprocate.

"What we had was pure, dad. Like you and ma. Wait, bro. Are you sitting on the faucet, like a little mini-dude?"

Chad's dad replied in the affirmative.

"I think she struggles without you, wraith bro."

"Wraith" was a word Chad's dad once taught him during their post-Twix and 'shrooms bath convos.

"Like, she be projecting a lot. On the C-Note."

Chad's therapist was always talking about projection.

"Sounds like some magical fairy chick rims that guy's ass every time he says it," Chad's meathead friend Ungar told Chad once when he said his therapist kept saying the word "project." Ungar didn't know what "project" meant. "You shouldn't listen to that part," he concluded. "Focus on everything else." He didn't want Chad to get ripped off.

"Dad, I never told you this, but I'm going to do it now, because I am going to keep it real with you, bro. I respect you sitting on my faucet. You could visit Tom Brady, but you visit me. That first time we went camping just us when I was thirteen, I went out from the cabin to drain the Chad vein. But I kept walking, bro. You had been yelling at me. You and ma weren't getting along. I even used to think that was the only reason you took me. You were asleep, so I just kept going and going.

There was this bear, right? And he was a big bastard. Like, on the bear football team, he'd be on the D-Line. Edge rusher. You knew how fast I was. And even somehow I knew that maybe I couldn't outrun this bear. And he starts walking towards me, but fast walking. Like in those horror movies when some bro is hauling ass and Jason is barely moving but he's gaining on this guy and he's gonna do him. Ha ha ha ta ha ha. Not like that, dad. Ha ha ta. You still so funny, bro. But this bear is gonna get me. But then this little moose dude comes out from behind a tree. I couldn't see him before that. And the bear jumps on him and he twists his neck around like three times like it was a steering wheel that didn't go back in the other direction and he bites into its shoulder and blood goes shooting up into the air and the entire time this bear mofo is staring at me as he does this. Like he wanted it to be me. And I went back to the cabin and you were still asleep and had a beer."

Chad's father's ghost said that sounded like projection.

"Bro, everybody be saying that word to me. That's what happens when you go to the movies, it's not what happens to you in real life. Duh."

Chad would try to hug it out with his father's ghost by gently cupping his hands together around the edges of the shadow on his shower faucet by his feet.

His cousin Tony C. once gave him a used knockoff Hitachi vibrator that had belonged to one of his girlfriends that Chad kept on his bathroom sink until he found something good to do with it.

Sometimes in the morning, after he had

climbed out of the cold water of the tub, he thought that maybe it threw a shadow on his shower faucet. Or else that his dad now lived in the Hitachi. "That's your second home, dad."

Either way, he kept it there.

CHAPTER 9
"Cosplay Convention"

"Broclops," a meathead named Chad said admiringly to his five foot, four inches tall neighbor, who was dressed up like Cyclops from the X-Men. "You are so cash money, bro. Ping ping pow!" It was time for Comic-Con, and Chad liked to talk in comic book sound effects.

Everyone called Chad's neighbor T. He was fifty. His regular name was Vinnie. So they called him T-Vin. Which was cool, because his last name was Tevant.

"T-Vin-T is in the house, bitches!" Chad was known to yell. Sometimes in T-Vin's apartment, where T-Vin's wife also was. That was where Chad liked to watch the Patriots win the Super Bowl.

He had a lucky spot on the couch by the cat's scratching post. And even though the cat was dead because T-Vin had gotten drunk and tried to see if it could swim in the harbor to settle a bet with Chad who had opined that the cat could swim, they kept the scratching post, because it was a lucky post.

T-Vin weighed three and a half bills. He also had played football in high school and was a great star. But there was more to this friendship than athletic glory. Both counted themselves among the superhero cognoscenti.

Once a year for Comic-Con Chad shaved his head and T-Vin painted Chad's head, his face, and his neck silver so that Chad could be the Silver Surfer. He had a surfboard made out of compacted Dunkin' Donut cups that he had gotten on eBay so he was a superhero who also stayed local and Dunkin' was the official coffee of the Patriots.

"There's like a lot of levels to what I do, T-Vin-T," Chad had said the first year he premiered his costume. "Like, I put the major on the major, right? You get that. But also the minor on the minor. It's like music, really."

T-Vin said very little. He was non-verbal. If his hands were in his pockets and you said, "'Sup, T-Vin," maybe one of his elbows would move a little like a turkey had had its wing blown a bit by an invisible hair dryer. But you had to be his boy to know what to look for.

"Whoosh, erronkkkk, thud thud!" Chad offered, by way of comic book sound effects, as the two hit the street and began their three-mile walk to the Hynes Convention Center in the Back Bay.

They always traveled by foot. Superheroes don't take the T. And the Surfer's board wouldn't fit in Chad's car, so he just pretended to ride it across town.

But the best part—even better than the actual Comic-Con—was when Chad would stop with T-Vin-T in the Public Garden. There would be many superheroes sitting on benches because the convention center was close.

They sat there in early spring, and Chad would brood on the old unknown world and how T.S. Eliot had written that April was the cruelest month, but we have a tendency to be indolent with our reading of those opening lines of "The Waste Land," because what Eliot actually means is that April is symbolically hard in that following the emotional dormancy of winter, and being numbed to life, we must come out again into the light, and that can be painful, nay, even cruel.

Clearly that did not happen.

Or did it, in a way?

Chad liked to watch the mallards in the Public Garden. They were so carefree. They didn't get to go inside and watch a lot of TV and that didn't bother them, and they were outside in the cold, and that did not bother them either.

"Bro, why are those ducks raping that other duck?"

They both watched. It was quite violent. Some ducks chased a single duck who kept flying away, but eventually she would have to stop to rest, and the raping ducks would jump on her.

T-Vin-T wasn't entirely non-verbal. Sometimes he could be roused. The Public Garden tended to bring out his philosophical side. Also, Cyclops had additional levels of sight compared to the average person.

"*Make Way for Ducklings,*" T-Vin-T said.

Chad gave him one of the blank stares he reserved for matters not having to do with football, superheroes, beer, subs, the value of protein, the essentiality of hydration, the demons that are carbs, or social solecisms—that is, the improper use of "bro," "chill," or handshakes without enough parts to them.

T-Vin-T explained that what you don't see in the popular children's book *Make Way for Ducklings* is that Pa Mallard rapes Ma Mallard, because that is what ducks do to breed.

"I'm a man, bro," Chad protested.

Chad did not know what T-Vin-T was getting at. But he knew something was way, way, way wrong here.

"You go on for now without me," Chad said nobly. "The Surfer needs to clear out this joint."

T-Vin-T said "whatever" and left.

Then Chad did what he had to do. He snuck up on a pile of those raping mallards and with his Dunkin' Donuts surfboard he lashed out, unleashing his powers.

"Splat, Gerong, ping ping pow!" he yelled. "Do it nice! Do it nice!"

After two hours he was exhausted and there were seven dead mallards scattered around the park. Three male, four female.

A mounted cop on a horse stood over Chad on a Public Garden bench by the suspension bridge.

"Suspect is detained," he said into his Walkie. "No, not a crazy homeless guy, actually. Drunken meathead. No, I know, it's new."

A Boston Police van showed up and Chad was ushered into the back after his blood-daubed and feather-festooned Dunkin' Donuts surfboard had been taken from him as evidence.

There was a smoking hot woman dressed up as Wonder Woman who was walking by with her boyfriend who was just an ordinary boyfriend as Chad got into the van.

"Today was about justice," was all he said.

Was all he had to say, you might say.

Fucking April, right?

CHAPTER 10
"Sensitivity Training"

Normally a meathead named Chad would have called the man who was helming his company's sensitivity training seminar "brother," but this was not going so well.

"Look, instructor, B, why can't we all just be beautiful with each other?"

"You are not allowed to gender people, Chad," the instructor had said as Chad's fellow employees, sitting in a circle, checked their phones.

"Bro?"

"Yes, like that."

"So just B?"

This was confusing. Bro was great. Everyone knew that. But you only said B for a special kind of Bro, and now this dude wanted Chad to automatically give everyone a B without them having to earn B-level status?

He said this. The instructor said it was not exactly what he meant.

"When you called Karen bro in the break-room, you triggered her because you gendered her. Karen doesn't identify as a male. And even if she does, you cannot presume gender."

Chad didn't even like Karen. He was just trying to be polite to get her to move from in front of the fridge where she was standing and peering in for like five minutes like she was Belichick studying game film and he just wanted to check on the status of his sub for when he ate it later.

"What am I supposed to say?" Chad asked.

"Can I ask her just to get her ass out of the way? Cool, bro. Shit, my bad. B. You all my B's." Whatever it took to end the meeting and turn down the heat when Chad just wanted to be cool in the kitchen of love or something like that. "I welcome you."

"I also have a problem with Chad," Chad's meathead friend Ungar said, after he raised his hand.

The instructor asked him to share.

"Well, when I was in the break room with Chad, he asked me what I thought about Sue and if I would hit that hard and I was like, 'Fellow employee, why you be disrespecting Sue like that you don't even know how she is gendered and if it would be appropriate for you to even hit that based upon her gender. You have to know the gender first, D-bag.'"

The instructor asked if anybody knew where

Ungar had gone wrong. Chad raised his hand as his fellow employees played games on their phones.

"First of all, B's, I would not do Sue like that. We tight. Not tight like a . . . in a . . . Shit. My bad."

He thought about making a few hand gestures, maybe with his thumb and forefinger in a circle, but decided against it. He could grow.

Once Sue had brought Chad a Dunkin' Donuts coffee with eighteen packets of Splenda in it like he liked when they were working late and he had not even asked her for a coffee.

"To power through our deadline," she had said and smiled and then they worked hard. Chad was happy to work hard that time. It felt like it had a point to it.

Then another time he brought her a coffee

without her having asked for it and it would go back and forth. Chad did not want anything to go wrong with Sue.

"I wouldn't want to hit that," he reaffirmed. "That's where the Ung Man is wrong. We're friends."

Sue was staring at the ground now instead of her phone. Chad feared that by "friends" everyone thought he was talking about Ungar and not Sue but everyone already knew he was friends with Ungar so hopefully Sue understood at least.

Ungar raised his hand again.

"Are you fucking kidding me, dude?" Chad interposed when he saw Ungar's hand go up. "This is so not cash money of you, Ung Man. Did you eat my fucking sub, too, because I will do you right here on this goddamn floor."

The instructor scribbled away furiously at

the piece of paper on the clipboard on his lap.

"Can I record this?" he asked Chad's boss, who was also playing with her phone. Ungar didn't wait for clearance from the instructor to speak.

"First of all, Chad just gendered me. Ta ha ha ha ta ha ha. He called me Ung Man. He shouldn't call me a man. Even though I am the Ung Man."

"Very good, Ungar," the instructor said, as he put his cell phone on a chair in the middle of the circle, with the recording app switched on.

"And then he said he was going to do me on the floor. I have not given consent."

"Also true," the instructor said.

Chad could handle no more.

"Look, I'm sorry, my bros. Wait: Sorry not sorry, my bros. Language isn't static."

He had learned that phrase from Sue late one night over Dunkin' Donut coffees as they worked on deadline. He looked at her now and she smiled back at him, and once more, God's little garden of hope began to bloom in Chad's heart.

"By do Ungar I meant beat the shit out of his wiseass bitch ass. And I don't mean bitch like he's a girl, I mean because he sucks sometimes, like when girls say bastard. I could have rolled with bastard. My love in my heart is equal for all of you. My hate in my heart is equal for all of you. It's just even, bros. .500 record. 8-8. Well, it's different with some. Like, maybe one of you is at 14-2, first round bye, home field advantage. But that's okay. That's . . . that's . . . " He wound up for it. " . . . That's . . . that's . . . life."

By this point, most of Chad's co-workers had left the conference room.

"Are we good until next month?" his boss asked the instructor, and the instructor said yeah they were.

Chad was sad that Sue had left early, but then he was happy when she was waiting in the break room with a Dunkin' Donuts coffee for him.

"Eighteen Splenda," she said, "Just how you like it."

And Chad thought, "Just how I like you, just how I like you."

CHAPTER 11
"Sports Radio"

"Ain't no need to be like that, bro," a meathead named Chad said to a man on the radio.

Chad called this man a lot. The man worked at the sports radio station Chad listened to every day. Chad was a regular caller and he liked to give his hot takes and most likely if he kept giving enough of them he would be offered a job at the radio station because they were so good.

"So you actually think it's smart to say that no one should care if NFL players get concussions?"

Chad sighed. Ignorance frustrated him, but

what could you do? That's how the world was now.

"What I'm saying, bro, is you get to play in the NFL. That's like you getting to be Christmas at the North Pole. So, like, if you take a risk or two, that's not really a risk any more than if you're with this hot girl, and you're like, okay, I got the hip control, I can disengage when I need to, I can say 'Hello, Mr. Stomach.'" Then he thought. "Mrs. Stomach."

Chad had improved at his calls over the years. At first they would have him on only for like fifteen seconds.

He could barely manage one sentence. There is fierce competition for the best air time.

He got it. It was like being a starting quarterback in the NFL. There were only so many jobs. Sometimes you had to wait for an opportunity like for someone to get hurt with a horrible injury and maybe snap a tibia and Chad sometimes hoped that something would happen to a bunch of the sports radio hosts so he could step up and get his chance.

That's how it was even for Tom Brady. Even Tom Brady had to wish for someone else to get hurt so he could do what he was meant to do.

"Life is real, bro," Chad would conclude with his inner voice—and sometimes his outer one, too, if the moment called for such gravity—when he thought about these matters.

"Life is like you going over the middle like Edelman and you know you're going to get popped and maybe almost swallow your tongue and forget your name for a bit, but when you remember your name again, your name might as well be Jesus because you are a savior and you might have saved the game if it was like fourth-and-twelve and you were down by three and there were less than twenty seconds to go and now you get to win. What could be wrong about that?"

Chad knew he was no stranger to deep thoughts. He ranked them. Early Metallica was the best band to lift to at the gym. You had to go golden oldie like that since weights themselves were golden oldies because metal had been around as long as humans had walked the earth.

"And I bet those Flintstone dudes who were the first people liked to throw rocks around and there was probably like some early version of Brady who had to deal with other shit like dinosaurs but he still stayed focused on his mission. Respect."

His thoughts on edging were also worth

savoring, but he didn't share them with many people. They stayed within his Temple of Chad.

Then there was a period when he'd drink a lot of wine and work on what he was going to say the next time on the sports radio station. At the wine store Chad would listen to the woman who worked there tell him about new bottles they had that she was excited about and how he could expect floral finishes, and chocolate finishes, and burnt orange finishes, and oak notes, late harvest blueberry notes, apple cinnamon touches.

He couldn't tell if she was flirting. So he kept going back to try and learn more. She sure said "finish" a lot. And she smiled every time she did. Maybe she also knew him from the radio. This is where it starts, he thought. Right here. Right now. From the Temple of Chad and then into the Gillette Stadium of the World.

That was where the Patriots played.

Chad's intentions were to pour himself a glass of wine all classy into something like his Star Wars coffee mug and not his big Dunkin' Donuts thermos, and to do what the woman at the wine store said.

Her name was Eve. She had said, "As in Adam and . . . " and Chad had said, "Vinatieri?" who was the greatest field goal kicker ever when he played for the Patriots. She laughed and called him witty. Anyway, her big thing was to "nose" the wine she had poured and that seemed like it only meant to smell it.

But after a couple glasses from the Darth Vader mug Chad would just drink the wine from the bottle because it was easier that way as he wrote his hot takes for the sports radio station.

Chad wasn't exactly aware that the hosts on the sports radio station were laughing at him. He understood that with greatness came jealousy. You think people didn't say shit to Brady, boy?

Chad said those very words one time on the radio and the host was African American though Chad did not know this. He got banned for a long time. He was just trying to be folksy. Like when his dad used to say to him, "You want the back of my hand, boy?" And: "Yeah, you had three goals, boy, but you missed two empty nets." And: "Help your ma with the dishes boy." And, sometimes, even, when Chad was very young: "I love you, boy."

There was nothing to do but buy more wine and keep trying.

Eve at the wine store said, "I haven't heard you on the radio in a long time. Their ratings must be plummeting without your hot takes."

So she knew after all. That explained so much.

Clearly it would be a great idea for them to get drunk together and have some deep convos.

"I have a heavy burden I carry around inside of me," Chad said.

"I have sensed that," Eve replied. "Your takes are not just hot. They are deep."

She was right. Anything deep was also heavy.

The wine store was more than just a wine store. Chad knew that he would always know that. He could do the math.

Deep = Heavy > Hot

Life doesn't give out A's for nothing. Or W's for wins.

Chapter 12
"Corner Café"

"Suppity sup, granbro," a meathead named Chad said to an old man named Rolston who sat outside the Caffé Dello Sport in the North End and drank espresso on Sundays.

"What's up yourself, you dumb meathead," Rolston said back.

Rolston was super old and he looked like a grape that had been dried in the sun so Chad called him Old Grapey.

He saw him every Sunday when he put on his Patriots shorts and his Celtics sweatshirt with the sleeves cut off to show the world his mighty guns regardless of if the sun was out or not.

Sometimes Old Grapey had an oxygen tank. But he literally always had an espresso and Chad ordered five at once in a single cup and they talked and Chad imagined he was Luke Skywalker and Old Grapey was Yoda.

"Grapey, why you be like always talking about olden days? Like when people cared about baseball and telling me about Mickey Mantle. Shit, bro. He wasn't even on the right team."

Old Grapey asked Chad what he was supposed to talk about with a dumbass like him but Chad always knew he was joking even when Old Grapey wasn't joking that much.

"Actually, Yodes, I can tell you a little something about love on this AM of ours this morning, yo yo yo. Nah, for realz. My baby girl Alysha. I call her Leesh. 'Cause her name is such a mouthful. Yeah, you feeling me. You on the ball. Ha ta ha ha ta. Now you double feeling me."

Chad felt sublimely witty. He didn't usually have it rolling like this.

"First when we met at the community center when I was balling, working on my reverse lay-lays, she comes over and says, 'I bet I can hand your ass to you if we go one on one, I'll even let you take the ball in first.' So I'm thinking she's never gonna touch it, and I start talking a little trash. 'Prepare to get penetrated, baby girl,' I says."

Old Grapey asked Chad what the hell was wrong with him.

"I don't know, O Wise One. Because when I took it to the hole—ta ha ha ta ha ta—she knocked the ball out, went straight up, laid it in—ta ha—and then she beat me bad, bro. So I was thinking like, 'Maybe she's not actually a girl,' but she was like really smoking, dude, and she teaches music so it ain't just sports and she said, 'Do you want to get a coffee,' and we came here and now she's my baby girl."

Chad and his Leesh did not talk music very much. He tried to get her into his "pump me up like a mofo" jams that featured in his sonic retinue—he did not use that phrase—at the gym, "but no dicey dice," as he told Old Grapey. He was a big boy. He could agree to disagree, not everyone has to love Whitesnake, they had enough fans.

She asked him when he left her place early Sunday mornings why he always had to go so early, and he said it wasn't because of another baby girl, which seemed to be more or less okay with her so he didn't say anything else.

"I want you to come with me," Old Grapey

said one morning.

Chad hadn't ever gone anywhere with Old Grapey and he had just gotten his five espressos but he said, "Sure deal, boss," which meant great solidarity.

They walked to the church around the corner. Old Grapey didn't have his oxygen tank that day.

"Come into the basement with me, you meathead," he said, and Chad laughed, but he was getting nervous.

In the basement there was a casket with an old woman in it.

"That's my wife, Chad," he said.

Old Grapey had never called Chad Chad before. Chad had forgotten Rolston's real name which he thought would be good to use here so he just said "bro" and touched his back but not in a way that Old Grapey would think was gay. It wasn't like that. It really wasn't.

After his visit with Old Grapey to the church, Chad minded it less when Leesh kicked his ass at basketball on the reg. He didn't see Rolston for a while so one day he went by his apartment.

"Big Chad checking in Big Chief. Hut huff huff." Chad was not the knocking type. Doors were meant to be opened. Old Grapey neither stirred nor blinked. He was sitting at his kitchen table with a mug of tea in front of him and listening to music.

"What'cha playin', Pops? Hanging in?"

Rolston told Chad that he was listening to Beethoven's late string quartets, and each time he did so he heard his wife's voice.

"Like, it talks to you?"

"Yes, it is like that," Old Grapey said, still neither blinking nor stirring.

Chad found this pretty concerning. Nay, scary. Nay, nay—super scary.

Maybe his old friend had the Alzheimer's and it would be a kindness to smother him and that was what Old Grapey was trying to say to Chad but did not know how to request this outright.

Chad was going to ask for clarification on the point, but then he listened hard to the music to see if he could hear the voice of Old Grapey's dead wife.

It didn't even sound like music.

It sounded like the air talking in all of the voices there had ever been, but clear, so clear, clearer than Chad thought even he could ever be, or anyone super smart, or Leesh who knew about music shit.

The next time Leesh and Chad played basketball and she said she was going to take him to the hole and make him her bitch, Chad said, Yo, wait, hold up, and asked her if she had ever heard Beethoven and his string quartets.

Old Grapey had had to say the name "Beethoven" and the term "late string quartets" like ten times each before he finally just grabbed Chad's phone from him at the Caffé Dello Sport, pulled out his credit card, and downloaded the music for him.

Meanwhile Leesh asked him why he was listening to Beethoven.

"I'm listening to you another way bigger than you or even me while we have each other," Chad replied.

That was the wisest thing she had ever heard anyone say.

"How did you come up with that?" she asked.

"Depends how you're spelling 'come' ha ha ha ta ha."

And so the mystery remained.

The mystery of Beethoven.

Or "B Bro," depending on how you spell it.

CHAPTER 13
"Freedom Trail"

"Time for you to get done, stone bro," a meathead named Chad said to a 220-foot-high granite obelisk perched upon a drumlin in Charlestown.

He was at the Bunker Hill Monument. It had 294 stairs, and Chad used it as one of his gyms.

He used many things as gyms. Like the roof deck of his apartment where he stripped down to his boxers and did push-ups even when people had parties there.

Chad was a warrior and a warrior always had to be ready to go. It wasn't just in love or in battle though those things could be more fun.

There were lots of people inside the Monument because it was on the Freedom Trail. Tourists from Texas, school kids on their field trips learning about the Revolutionary War, lots of Asians from China, but only Chad, mighty he, ran up and down the Monument stairs over and over again.

He chanted "Zulu Zulu Zulu," and many people filmed Chad on their phones for this and other reasons and sometimes he went viral for what he said and did in these stony confines but a warrior cannot become distracted.

He even had a ranking system because he was not a puss, and though Chad hated cats because he thought they were bad dead people in animal form, that was not what he meant by puss.

1-2 straight climbs and you were a Zulu

intern. That sucked. Even at work Chad was not an intern.

3-4 and you were a Zulu back-up which was a little better but still pretty shameful.

5-7 climbs and you were a Zulu warrior and now we were talking. You were sexy, you were golden, your body was hot bronze and gold.

8-9 and you were a Zulu king. You had many wives and your wives could be the girls you saw in the Monument who were bent over trying to catch their breath like they were waiting for you.

10-12 and you were a Zulu emperor. The Monument and the surrounding lands were yours. People knew your name and wanted to scream it out if you were kind enough to follow them home and go into their bedroom with them and even their husbands would be like, "I defer to you, Zulu emperor Chad."

His record was 12, obviously.

The tourists from Texas would see Chad running up the stairs and tell him he was not going to make it, he needed to pace himself, and Chad, caught in Chadian throes of passion, would say, "Pace this, bitches," and grab his own ass—it felt so fine—as he blew past.

He considered the Monument a symbol of what it meant to be fit and big and good. It penetrated the sky. Chad didn't just admire this manly structure, he went inside of it, and when he was inside of it it also felt like it was inside of him and they were inside of each other in a really gratifying way that he hoped was mutual because he liked to take care of his bros like that.

"I got you, stone bro."

People were often in Chad's way but he would not budge even if he had to mow them down.

"It's just like driving, bro, right-hand lane," he would say alike to suburban housewives and some French hipster he wanted to disembowel and a haunted-eyed school child from Taunton.

Sometimes he saw an overweight set of parents at the top, trying desperately to catch their wind.

Their kid might say, "Mommy, that man is going up and down, again and again," and Chad would say, "Come with me, little bro, let me teach you the right way to do things," and he would stick out his mighty jaw towards these lackluster parents. Damn Chad felt fit in the Monument and if he wanted to eat four éclairs after he would still look like the bomb. Between desperate heavings of breath the parents said, "Do you believe this asshole?"

and Chad would say, "Yeah, yeah I do."

Little Jimmy went with Chad back down to the bottom, but he'd only make it back up 25 stairs and the Zulu warrior would say, "Later, dead weight," and power on, because that was what ZW's did.

Fit women commented on Chad's calves a lot. A mega-lot. He only wore shorts, just like he only did rooftop push-ups in boxers.

"Nice definition," one said, pointing.

You know it.

Another said, "I wish my calves looked like yours."

Yeah, she was feeling it.

She could have felt it for real, Chad thought. The Aquarium had a touch tank. You touched starfish. Chad's calves could be like that.

"Starfish, ta ha ha ha ha ta ha."

Man he was mirthful and witty when he was

in battle mode.

So many fit women started saying things about Chad's legs that he thought he'd get in on the game and start saying things about theirs.

"Damn those legs are sweet, yo," he said to a woman with a Southern accent who had a Duke sweatshirt on. She probably went there. That was hot.

Lots of complaints were filed and a female park ranger confronted Chad at the bottom of the Monument and said he would be banned if he did not stop his suggestive comments.

He looked her up and down. There was nothing to say here. So he just said, "You should try some climbs, bro."

CHAPTER 14
"Fortune Teller"

"Whoa whoa whoa, madame bro," a meathead named Chad said to a fortune teller.

"Is that really what you see? Is that to be my fate?"

"O no."

"O whoa is me."

"Whoa whoa is Chad."

Thus concluded Chad's lamentations.

This fortune teller came highly recommended.

She was the aunt of Chad's meathead friend Ungar. The Ung Man had realized the C-Note had been down and thought it would help to know things would get better someday.

"I am feeling you, bro," Ungar had said. "I know Alysha was your baby girl but she is gone now and your forever baby girl will a different girl be."

Shit Ungar read a lot. That's how he could talk like a faucet you turned on and golden streams of words came out.

"Not like piss, bro," Chad clarified. He was very down/sad.

"No, I get it, Note," Ungar conciliated, and he punched Chad hard in Chad's bicep four times, because that was what you did when you were tight.

"It's not good, what I see. It's no good," Madame Fabula said, squinting her eyes and pinching her chin and looking at the conch shell which was sometimes an ashtray on her kitchen table.

"Shit, Mad bro, are you seeing ghosts?" Chad wisely inquired. " 'Cause I think ghosts follow me. I am a haunted man, MF. Wait. Ta ha ha ha ta ha. MF. I am cursed. I am not mean to old people and I go to a job and I know I am blessed with the Patriots and Brady but there is a hole in me, and whenever I dump things into me because I want to be filled and loved like anyone else, it's like it goes out the hole. Are you picking up what I am putting down? Please tell me you are. Please." He was going to wail like when he was certain he had cold cuts but the cold cuts were all gone and the store was closed.

The fortune teller adjusted her sweatshirt and her sweatpants. It was hot without the AC working and this guy in her kitchen smelled like a steak and cheese sub.

"The ghosts are real," she said, and Chad

let loose a mighty moan.

"Your past eats your future happiness. The ghosts of the past feast. Accept your past and the people from it. Square your accounts with them in your mind, and come back next week."

Damn she wanted a sub now. Chad had that effect on people.

That night Chad got very drunk in his bathroom. He didn't always get malt liquor but when he did he meant business. He had been baptized, he had made his first communion, and he understood that drinking malt liquor because you had to break down walls in your mind was like a sacrament and it was holy in an adult way.

"The Church of Real Life," as Chad put it, and he drank and stared at his phone for what he knew he must do.

In college Chad was a football star and he hooked up with lots of girls, but only one girl hooked up with his heart.

That was Lesley. Everyone called her Laz. "Because she is a spaz," improvised Chad. "On my curtain rod"—because he was prone to bouts of associative imagery.

He called. He waited. He knew, somehow, that she would know it was he. Children were audible in the background as she answered and said, "You cannot be calling here," and then asked if he was drunk.

"Drunk for you, Laz. Let us make it right. The time is now. Do it now. Carps gonna get diemed."

The malt made him quite deep. May it make you half so deep should you ever have occasion to sip its nectar and mull.

He decided to take her back in his way-back

machine. They had humped behind a table in Cancun on spring break while people were gathered around. They had humped on the roof of her building after he had cheated on her and they were together again celebrating in nature. There had been a bus hump when she took him to meet her pops. But he could not remember if it was she whom he humped in the bathroom of an academic building at school as the students filed past outside. But he did remember exclaiming, "Tell them to work harder, tell them to work harder," whomever he had been humping.

Beauty was so potent.

"That was you, wasn't it Laz? Who else could it have been?"

She said that it could have been a lot of people, asked once more if he was drunk, and called him a selfish dick who needed to get his life together.

So it was true.

She did still care.

Madame Fabula was right about getting his past in order and finding a girlfriend from that past. Maybe the husband could take the kids. Chad would be the new husband now. Not legally. He would have to see how it went. Laz was a spaz after all.

He could not hear the kids anymore. They must have gone into a different room. Now they could talk proper.

Laz told Chad that he had hurt her so much. She was a principal at a middle school now and she tried to stop kids who were like Chad from going on to become adult Chads. In a way he helped her find a career so he didn't appreciate having his spot blown up like that.

"And you just used me. You never even

cared about me."

Chad countered her doleful claim with powerful emotion.

"Awww. Come on, bro."

"We broke up, and I had to go to therapy like twice a week, and you got your friends to make fun of me, and I had an eating disorder, and you had a name for me. How can you not remember this, you drunk stupid asshole? You called me Satan. Never call here again and get help."

She hung up. Chad bellowed into his phone. It was his version of Whitman's barbaric yawp, only much, much, much more buzz killed.

"I love you Satan!!!!!!"

Well, that was done. Madame Fabula had tricked him and brought the devil into his life. But wait. Maybe the devil was a ghost hunter because you never heard jack about there being ghosts in hell and the ghosts would be gone now.

Huh.

He'd have to see.

CHAPTER 15
"Art School"

"Did you 'drate today, bro?" a meathead named Chad asked his fourteen-year-old neighbor Remy after she had asked him a confusing question.

By "'drate," Chad meant, of course, "hydrate." Fluids were very important to him, as they are to all members of the meathead brethren. "'Cause I don't know why you be asking me this," he continued.

They were in the hallway of their building. Remy was the daughter of Chad's friend who was named Vinnie but everyone called him T for some reason, so he was T-Vin, and his last name was Tevant so Chad called him T-Vin-T, which sounded like the stuff that blew other stuff up.

Remy tried to explain again.

"My mom has parent-teacher meetings at her school in Concord. My dad has AA and he cannot miss this one." Remy also spoke French, German, and a little Polish. But she also spoke Chad. "Or his sponsor be like mad pissed homie." Oh. That clarified matters. "And it's art exhibition night at my school and I can only go if an adult takes me and I want to see my painting in the exhibit."

Remy's school was not an ordinary school. It was a school for little artists. So Chad was a little nervous but he did not hate himself for it and it did not make him want to cut himself like some other things did and had before because even Tom Brady still got nervous at the ends of games when the Patriots could lose—not like they were really going to lose. And not like Chad would either. He'd take one hard for his team when he had to and Remy was on his team. Team Chad.

"So you'll do it?"

He stuck out his lower jaw which was his go-to pose to indicate strength, sacrifice, or when he was about to cum.

"I will, girl bro."

"I love you, Uncle Chad," Remy replied, and hugged him around the bellybutton, because that was all she came up to.

"Just Chad," Chad said, because the term uncle made him feel old.

"JC," the child replied, and Chad thought of another JC, and understood much, and understood much indeed.

In a way, Remy was almost his. T-Vin's wife

always liked Chad and they hooked up in the basement where the laundry machine was when she was a little bit pregnant with Remy—Chad didn't like "too pregnant," if you know what we mean—so maybe a little bit of him got in there. That was a tough time in T-Vin's life, so while he wouldn't have said this aloud, in a way, kinda/sorta, Chad was doing everyone a solid.

His heart pounded in the school parking lot. It was night. He didn't like going to schools at night. Smart-dressed kids with smart-dressed parents walked with purpose towards the entrance. Chad had on his best Patriots sweat-shirt—it was his 1980s throwback model and this one still had sleeves—but he didn't know, man, he didn't know. This was not his scene.

"Don't be nervous, JC bro," Remy said. "Art is fun and I want you to see my painting." Then she said something that blew Chad's mind. He wasn't ready for it, really. But nobody could have been ready for it.

"I care what you think," Remy concluded.

The paintings were really great, Chad could see. He couldn't see lines, "per say"—a phrase he wrote a lot in work emails when he had to be on his smart game—but if there were lines he was pretty sure that everyone stayed within them, and that was half the painting battle.

"In this room are non-representational paintings," Remy said, leading him into a classroom across from a small gym. He looked longingly through the tiny rectangular windows of the gym door. Oh how easier that would have been! Remy did not play sports, but, oddly, as Chad mulled in this moment, he still had affection for her. He probably wouldn't even have had more if she was a girl quarterback. Cray but mostly true.

Chad did not understand the non-representational paintings very well. They weren't even of anything. They were just fucking colors. He wanted to smash some of them. But they also reminded him of the cards one of his very first therapists would hold up in front of him when he was six and he was supposed to say what he saw in the shapes of the drawings on the fronts.

"That's a football, that's my mom's head under the wheel of a bus, that's me getting in trouble again and my dad telling me how I do bad, that's Santa's Village," and so forth.

So that relaxed him a little.

They came to the room where Remy's painting was. Many kids and parents and what Chad figured were teachers—you could always spot a teacher—were gathered around it. Chad was taller than everyone so he could look from the back.

In the painting was a man who maybe looked a little like Chad. He was sitting on top of a great round boulder on top of a grassy hill. For some reason it looked as if the man had rolled the boulder there. Maybe because the grass going up the hill was crushed down like the boulder had made a path. The man was smiling. His flat right hand was above his eyes so he could see better in the sun and he was looking out over the far side of the hill that he had not already gone up like he was excited about seeing what was on the other side.

"It is deliciously absurd," he heard a voice say. "It flirts with the non-representational," said another.

That was enough for JC.

"Hold up, bros. Ain't nothing absurd about this. And it sure as hell represents. It represents big time. You cannot represent more."

A woman whose heart was in the right place asked Chad what it represented.

We all have moments—though we may have but few of them—when we are not as we were. But we are still as we have been. Somewhere. There is a difference.

"It represents . . . it represents . . . the indomitable human spirit and what it must necessarily endure to be truly alive."

What a great night for both of them.

Chad could hardly believe it.

They rode back in silence. Glowing. Outside of Chad's door, because T-Vin-T, T-Vin-T's wife, and Remy all lived one floor up, the painter gave the art critic a hard hug around the bellybutton as they said goodnight.

"You got my painting," she said.

"I got you," he replied, and that night he did not get drunk at all, he just 'drated.

Chapter 16
"Writing Class"

"Yeah, I'm up for some brose," a meathead named Chad thought to himself, believing, as was his wont, that "brose" was an immaculate pun upon the word prose. "Gonna do some pieces. Ta ha ha ha ta ha."

When it comes to the world of literary arts, any meathead worth his salt—not that he wants to have too much sodium, because it dehydrates you and hydration is King—knows that you are supposed to say the words "prose" and "piece" a lot, and you cannot go wrong.

Besides, "prose" only meant sentences. And people talked about it like it was complicated.

With the arrival of spring, and given that he had not had a baby girl in a while to feel him and pick up what he was putting down, Chad decided to take a writing class at the local adult learning center.

He wrote mad stories in middle school with lots of dark caves in them and holes people never got out of and foot binding, so he thought naturally he would excel.

Plus, you only had to bring a notebook and now your phone could be a notebook so you didn't have to bring anything really.

The teacher wasn't mad hot but she was cool and she had a blog and Chad thought he should get a blog someday for his deep thoughts because he also wanted to be less selfish and right now he wasn't helping the world by keeping all of those thoughts in the Chad Bank, by which he meant his head.

"So now that we've all read Edgar Allan Poe's 'The Tell-Tale Heart,' I hope you are not all too plagued by guilt."

Everybody laughed, so when Chad heard and saw this, he thought he better laugh too, but things had definitely taken a dark turn and it was time to be on his guard. Like a panther in one of the caves of his middle school stories who ate this kid who wandered in from outside with a stick after his parents had told him he screwed up again when he didn't do nothing. The panther killed that kid. Chad shuddered. What if the panther had not been ready?

Exactly.

The teacher said that each of the students for next time would write and read a short eight-hundred-word piece—which did not sound very short to Chad, it sounded like something out of the Bible—that had something to do with guilt.

"It can be fantasy, it can be horror, it can be social realism, it can be some new mode of storytelling you've invented just for us, like a post-postmodern satire about a meathead to unite a divided country and show we are not as different from group to group as we tend to think."

More laughter. And again, Chad thought of the panther and how he had to be like one.

Chad worked hard on his piece with his prose. He even read the Poe story. That guy kind of seemed like a pussy and a stupid one, too. Chad did not approve of the brainless.

"Bro should have just thrown the heart into the ocean or gone to a zoo and fed a lion."

He wasn't even sure the guy that Poe reported about was even worthy of being called bro.

Thoughts for a rainy day.

"April showers bring May flowers" was one of Chad's favorite sayings, and he said it often inside of the Chad Bank. It echoed off the steel walls and that felt nice.

Plus, he wanted to hook up with this girl named Jessie in the class. But deep hook up. With love. That lasted. Forever. Or through the summer. It sucked to be alone in the summer.

He should have known the teacher would call on him first. It always went that way. But he was ready. His prose was ready for battle.

"Panther prose bros."

So he began to read his story about a boy who gets in trouble because he lied about why the sock was under his bed.

"I didn't do nothing, Ma," said the boy. "It just got lost."

"Then why is it so hard and crusty?" Ma replied.

You got the sense from the story that the Ma character was kind of trying to be funny, but maybe the kid didn't get her humor.

But this was just the first part. Because the boy grew up. He still had some of his guilt of the sock. The sock was his tell-tale heart. He was drawn, drawn, drawn back to the house where the bed had been with the sock under it.

He was ravaged by time, by his suffering. He drank and he drank as he was drawn and he was drawn, back to the house, and though there were many cars outside, he went in, to face his past.

And there was Ma, with the ghost of his pops, hovering behind so many people waiting for him in a circle, his friend Ungar and his friend Trey, and his neighbor everyone called T-Vin, and some chicks from work, and his old gym teacher **Mr.** Perrie, and there was a chair for him.

It appeared he would have to answer for the sock. But no.

"We need to talk about your drinking, son," said the Ghost of his Father, and all assented in a great, final, murmur of truth.

The End.

The reading of the prose in Chad's piece left him too drained to focus on what anyone else read, and he also didn't care that much.

But after the class was over, Jessie approached him.

"Do you know how real you are?" she inquired. "Do you know how tonally authentic you are within fictive spaces?"

In other times, on other days, with other

muses, Chad would have said, "Natch." But that would not do here.

So he said, "Naturally," they got lattes at the Starbucks around the corner, and they had a nice—well, nice-ish—summer.

CHAPTER 17
"Corn Maze"

"Ta ha ha ta ha, of course I can drive a Brotractor, boss," a meathead named Chad said to a farmer who was now seriously doubting if he should have hired this man for weekend help.

"Can you or can you not drive a tractor?" the man asked by way of clarification.

Math was involved in the assembly of any vehicle, Chad knew, hence his cool pun—something he did not do a lot of, but now this boss dude was annoyed and Chad felt like he didn't do nothing.

Chad was trying to extend his radius. That

was the term his therapist used.

"You just see these same people, don't you? They seem very similar to you in terms of their interests."

Chad pondered for a moment.

"We all like the Patriots. But everyone likes them."

The therapist said that he did not like the Patriots and Chad was aghast. There was only one thing to say.

"Bro?"

"I root for my patients," Chad's therapist concluded.

Well, whatever. Chad just hoped he was the starting quarterback.

So he took a job for a few weekends in early autumn at a farm in Ipswich. He was going to make the corn maze that children would play in, which was cool, because Chad was a big autumn buff.

When someone asked him once if he was an autumn buff Chad laughed because that was not what buff meant but this girl was cute and he wanted her to like him so he didn't call her stupid but she thought he was so she just said she had a boyfriend and Chad did not even get a chance to try and break them up.

Obviously that sucked.

"Don't make the maze too complicated," the boss bro said and Chad said, "Sure, bross," which was the funniest thing he had concocted in about a week, but the bross either did not hear this or care so he just continued. "And make sure you leave Lucy alone."

"Awww, shit," Chad thought. "Another bross with another daughter who is gonna be wanting the Radness of his Chadness."

Fresh autumn air out in nature made him

confident.

"Here she comes now," said the bross, and out from the barn walked a black German shepherd wearing a vest that said, "Dog with a Job."

"Come'ere girl, hut huff huff. Come'ere girl, hut huff huff," Chad beckoned, but no dice, so he caught the keys the bross flipped him and set to business.

Sometimes Chad had to help pick the apples on the farm because he ate lots of cider donuts and ran up a tab that he had to pay off. He excelled at getting big hunks of food in his mouth in a single bite and so the donut count mounted because they were like potato chips to a growing man like Chad.

But wait. Because then Chad was triggered by a donut. As he rode on the tractor crushing ears of corn while he plowed ("ta ha ha ta ha") his paths in the developing maze, he thought of a party he went to in sixth grade. There was a smart girl named Amy Liu and Chad was an autumn buff so it was his time to shine because the party had a harvest theme.

But when it was his turn to bob for apples he came up with two in his mouth at once. Truth was, there was room for a third and everyone laughed because who the hell had a mouth that big?

"My mouth can do more than get a lot of apples in it," he said later privately to Amy Liu, who said, "Gross, disgusting, yuck," but Chad had not meant it that way, he had meant that talking would be good if she wanted to sometime.

He cried as he drove the tractor, then he realized he needed support. He could not go it alone out here in the wilderness. The bross and his family had left to go to the bross' kid's soccer game. Chad felt very abandoned.

"Come'ere girl," Chad pleaded, "come'ere, Lucy." The dog's name sounded like the last name of the girl he knew all those years later as Apple Girl. She cut his apple open, and it was true: that seed inside really was a heart when you sliced the apple in two.

The faithful dog hopped atop the tractor, and the two rode.

"You feeling me, girl? You feeling me?"

And the dog panted.

She was feeling him, Chad concluded.

Dogs get it.

But then Lucy must have smelled something, or wanted to get away from the man who would lay down his life—well, it depends what else was going on—to protect her, and she ran off.

Chad called and he called, but the dog would not return. She howled. She could not find him. She was lost in the maze and scared and starving and there was no water in a corn field. So Chad did what he had to do. He cut the apple in half, no matter the cost to him personally.

By which we mean, he ran over almost every last corn stalk, destroying the maze and the crop, until he found the dog, who wasn't in the maze at all by then, but in its little dog house outside of the barn.

O well. These things happen. It is best to be a noble of purpose, if not the architect of the perfect ending.

"My bad, bross," Chad said to the farmer, when the farmer and his family had returned from the soccer game and the farmer had seen what Chad had done to his number one attraction.

Chad thought his radius had probably closed, if that's what a radius did.

"I escaped my maze tonight, bro," Chad said, as he flipped the farmer the keys. "I never asked to be put in it. I never asked at all."

He would miss those donuts, though.

"Bronuts. Ta ha ha ta ha ha."

CHAPTER 18
"Beaver Pond"

"Hide yourself, Bucky bro, or they're gonna get you," a meathead named Chad said to a beaver who had surfaced just outside of his dam.

This was not a job Chad enjoyed.

His friend Trey wanted to find this beaver and kill it. The beaver lived in a kettle pond behind Trey's house and as Chad understood matters the beaver liked to turn the pond into a waterpark that caused Trey's backyard to flood and then his basement. So Trey proposed that Chad come over with their meathead friend Ungar and Chad's neighbor Vinnie whom everyone called T for some reason and whose last name was Tevant and who went by T-Vin-T.

"We will get drunk, bros," Trey had said, "and hunt that mofo and fuel up with some burgers because beavers are tricky bastards and can stay underwater for days like fish."

Chad said that maybe they could catch the beaver and set it free somewhere else or else chain it to a tree near the dog house that Trey's dog lived in so the dog could have a friend and they could have a mascot for Patriots games.

Chad was always for the humane solution.

"I'm like for the humane solution, bro," Chad concluded. "And, you know, like, beaver. Ta ha ha ha ta ha."

They all laughed that most euphonic brand of laughter they knew so well from their days as hale fellows well met.

Actually, Chad had a fondness for beavers. One had bitten him as a kid. It was a baby beaver and it was on the land and Chad pulled the beaver's tail. The baby beaver tried to get away, but Chad kept pulling it and after the fifteenth or sixteenth pull it turned around and bit Chad's thumb and made it bleed, but Chad respected that the beaver had waited so long and was cool with playing for a good stretch at first.

Other animals would have been dicks about that. They didn't get it. They just wanted to be animals, but even for animals Chad knew there was more to life and he thought of them as good friends and if he were an animal it was reasonable to think that he would be a beaver.

Like a beaver would be a Patriots fan if beavers had TVs because they had dens they sat in. Kind of like a Man Cave. And when they were in their dens they ate sticks they had stored up while they relaxed which was a lot like eating potato chips and the Cape Cod kind was Chad's favorite.

Once he had gone to a zoo and fed some Cape Cod chips to a river otter and the river otter ate it all and river otters were pretty close to beavers but thinner.

"I'm not feeling this, Ung Man," Chad said to his friend Ungar as they crept around the pond with their BB guns ready to fire or to protect themselves in case they were attacked. "I am not comfortable making this beaver my bitch."

Chad raised a good point.

"Give me a second to think," the Ung Man proposed, so Chad continued as they both took enormous sips of beer and Chad wondered if a sip could be enormous or should you call it something else. He normally liked to just keep one thing on his mind at once.

"I say we find this bro, let him drink all of the beer he wants, then after when he passes out we pick him up, put him in the Chad Mobile, and we just say we couldn't find him and it's late so we have to go and we'll leave him on the side of the road somewhere."

Ungar agreed that this was a capital plan.

But then Ungar went inside Trey's house where Trey and T-V-Tin were watching college football and Ungar didn't just use the bathroom but he also started watching college football and got very drunk and fell asleep as Chad walked the woods alone.

At last he found his quarry, sitting on a felled tree, eating a big chunk of wood like it was a tasty slice of pizza.

The beaver did not seem very concerned about Chad's gun. But Chad had come in peace, so he threw the gun in the water, ruining it.

"So we meet again," Chad began, and he sat not far from the beaver, who continued to eat his slice of wood.

"I get you, bro, you fueling up."

Chad wished he had a Twix or an energy drink. My kingdom, my kingdom for an energy drink, as the old song went.

He thought of the beaver whose tail he once pulled, who let him play with him fifteen or sixteen times before he finally said "enough" and bit Chad and made his thumb bleed so that Chad would know the game was complete.

"I feel connected to you, bro," Chad said, but the beaver winced hard, dropping its slice of wood as it took a BB to its left shoulder, and scampered off away from the pond and into a thicket of underbrush.

It was the Ung Man and his smoking gun bringing Chad a six-pack of the Natural Light.

"Sorry, bro, was I cock-blocking you with that beaver?" the Ung Man asked, perhaps inevitably.

"You killed that bitch, bro, ta ha ha ta ha ha," Chad said to Unger, and then they both told Trey that that bitch had been done Ung Man-style so it was game over out at the pond, but Chad knew the little fella was a battler and would probably make it.

It was very late when it was time for Chad to get into his car and drive home drunk. But he could feel the love in the woods.

He turned towards the pond, and said what anyone who understood nature like Chad understood nature would say.

"Stay free, bro, stay free."

Then he drove really carefully.

Chapter 19
"Suicide Hotline"

"Hang on, bro, you climb that rope, you don't fall off of it," a meathead named Chad said to a woman who was thinking about killing herself and had called the suicide hotline.

"We got you, bro. I am on the line. Your life line. And I can feel your pulse. Stay with me."

They didn't say you had to use the phrase "stay with me" a lot during the training program, but Chad generally favored it.

The suicide prevention line was a good way to meet people and to give back to his community which was the Patriots way and Chad loved the Patriots.

"What is your name, baby girl?" Chad asked in his most soothing tone.

"My name is Cate with a C," came the reply. "And aren't you not supposed to gender people who call?"

"Life genders people, baby girl. We are all equal in suicide. I got you. Now please tell me your problem. You can go slow. I am not going to yell. If you want to just stay on the phone and not talk I have snacks. Granola, some energy bars to fuel up for the gym later, a sub that is the bomb, and obviously I have lots of energy drinks and water so I can hydrate, or 'drate as we say in the medical business. There is no pressure on you. This is about taking the pressure off of your heart. You feeling me?"

Cate told Chad that she used to work at the suicide hotline center.

"I never thought I would be one of those

people," she said. "It's like F. Scott Fitzgerald said, 'Life is something you dominate if you're any good at it.' I couldn't see it starting to dominate me."

Chad was not a man who got jealous much. He knew what he had going on. Or he was good at pretending, and how you pretended decided a lot about if you would do good in life or not. Still . . .

"This Scott dude works here? Did you guys hook up?"

Cate with a C laughed.

"You are funny," she said. "You are so bad at this but I have not laughed in I don't even know how long. Even if you clearly skipped the training program."

Chad was going to add that he trained himself yo yo yo, but instead he pointed out that they were both fellow C-Dawgs.

"Arfff arff arff," he added.

"I've taken a lot of pills I probably shouldn't have. Can you maybe call someone?"

Chad snapped his fingers and the sound seemed to echo through the call center.

He pretended he was Coach Belichick of the Patriots trying to get a referee's attention so that he could throw the red challenge flag.

The game was on the line, and this call needed to be reversed. A red challenge flag to Death.

"I will keep talking to you, baby girl, in my special way, so that you do not fall asleep and are pumped and jacked because I will not let hot Death blow up your spot."

A supervisor came to Chad's chair.

"This girl bro needs an ambulance STATS," he said, without cupping his hand over the phone, and believing that STATS meant statistics like passer rating and touchdown-to-interception ratio.

"I am going to get real with you, other C-Dawg," he said, now that the ambulance had been dispatched.

"I seem like I have it all, sure. But I get how life is like another set of reps when you haven't fueled up and you are not 'drated. I get it. I kick back in the tub sometimes and I'm looking at my body, and my body is to die for . . . Shit . . . my bad. My body is to live for, you feeling me, and even with what I'm seeing I see that razor blade and I think, 'There can be more than water in this tub,' right, and I won't have to pretend anymore and I can go to a place where what I am is not just like fine but like Tom Brady super fine. So then I just get really drunk. And that helps me. And if I ate too much, that helps me too because I heave, and then I just rip it at the gym the next day, harder than ever, because maybe then next time in my tub I'll just be thinking about my body and how I would be fucked yo without it. We ain't nothing without our bodies."

It was beautiful, and he felt like praying. That happened a bunch but instead he cracked an energy drink.

"You seeing anyone, baby girl?"

Cate with a C answered that she had gone through a string of dicks.

"Ta ha ha ta ha ha ta ha," said Chad.

"How about you?" Cate asked.

"I have been through a box of bitches," Chad replied. It was good to speak in the caller's terms, Chad's supervisor had said.

The truth is, Chad did not have awesome STATS in the whole people calling and not-then-dying game.

His meathead friend Ungar worked there, too, and Ungar was saving people left and right so Chad really did not want this girl to kill herself.

It was time to be very cash money.

"Life is like a rope in gym class," he began. "Yeah, you could just let go, you could fall to the floor in front of your classmate bros and break your spine and die or be a cripple and want to be dead instead. Or you can climb that rope, and it feels good. It can feel damn good. Like magical feeling good."

Chad's first orgasm had been in gym class. He told Ungar that it happened when he was seven but Ungar did not believe him and besides, Ungar had been six he said and that was the record. "That babysitter's hand didn't know what hit it," proclaimed the Ung Man.

Chad could hear the ambulance outside of

the place where Cate with a C lived. It was time to wrap this up and let the healing begin.

"I love you," he said. "The C-Note loves you."

All of a sudden Cate with a C sounded very alert and quite alive at that.

"Did you just call yourself the C-Note?"

"You feeling me, bro."

"I think we hooked up. You never called after."

Chad said nah.

"Do you have a Patriots comforter?"

He could hear the paramedics in her apartment now.

"Hook up with life, other C-Dawg. Hook up with life."

And he hung up.

Then he remembered the caller was supposed to hang up first.

"My bad, dawg," he said to the air.

CHAPTER 20
"Other Places"

"We are entering the atmosphere of Brogon6969," said a ship's command voice to a meathead named Chad. "We will drop you off."

"Cool, bro," replied Chad as he awoke. Wait. Was he dead?

He was not. But the rest of Earth, as he had known it, if he had ever really known anything about any of it, was. The post-human phase of Man's—and Woman's (and everyone else's)—existence had dawned.

A chip was put in his brain, and he would understand what was happening, for the most part, because the universe probably had better things to do than debrief Chad.

But eh. Who knows.

Thus, Chad understood that there was some kind of Noah's Ark deal going on. And when he asked inside of his head what Noah's Ark was, the answer was provided for him, because previously Chad had believed an ark was something related to a Tom Brady pass thrown deep down the field with a lot of touch and altitude.

Everyone who was the best ever at what they did had been gathered by higher beings to occupy worlds like Brogon6969, and it did not matter if they died a very long time ago or not because the beings who decide these things were sick and fucking tired of watching what went on on earth.

"Screw this, bro," one alien who ranked at the upper levels of management said to another, and that other one said, "I am picking up what you are putting down."

Chad was transported as if by magic atop the fertile surface of Brogon. He didn't really recognize anyone, but then he saw John Lennon, who he understood was the best Beatle so that was why he was here.

"Bro-bag," Lennon said, giving Chad a hard punch in his bicep like his meathead friend Ungar did back on earth before the aliens did the right thing and ended that bitch.

Chad was ready to make his first friend. Shit he had a good line.

"Love is all you need, bro."

Lennon just stared at him, so Chad continued, as had been his general practice on earth.

"Or like a condom ta ha ha ha ta ha ta ha."

Still Lennon stared.

"Or protein. You feeling me, Lennon? Did

you bring any girls?"

Lennon had not brought any girls. It was not his decision who got to come and who did not, as he informed Chad, who then laughed ceaselessly until Lennon walked away.

There were more people Chad did not recognize, but each time he asked inside his brain, "Who the fuck is that?" his brain answered him on account of the chip that had been planted in his one lobe that seemed to give the aliens anything with which to work. ("Is this one literally made of salami?" had been a popular joke making the alien rounds.)

Billie Holiday was there because she was the best at singing jazz and Chad thought she was hot so he asked her out and she said please, life is too short, which was strange because Chad was under the impression it was neither short nor long here on Brogon and it just went on and on and you couldn't tell if that was bad or good or if it sucked and Chad was scared he could not feel anything.

"Help Van Gogh bro," he said to the painter, laughing because Chad was so good at rhymes and he was not going to allow his spirit to be quashed.

Van Gogh had the VD and so did Chad so they talked about that for a while until Shakespeare came by and Chad said, "Whoa, bro, how come I can understand you?"

"Dude," Shakespeare said, "we all got the chip, right? And it just converts each of us into each other's wavelengths so if you ain't be feeling me I just make you my bitch until you do. Dig?"

These guys were okay. He saw the ghost of his pops because his pops' ghost was the best dad ghost there was apparently, and that was reassuring. But they didn't have anything to say to each other. Not everything changes because you move to another planet.

Sure, there were sub shops everywhere, and rivers of energy drinks, and a giant statue of Tom Brady that must have been a thousand feet tall but no Tom Brady himself because he had been moved to somewhere else that wasn't Brogon6969.

But Chad was the best at what he did, and he came to accept his greatness, though the mantle lay heavy upon him, as greatness always does upon the truly great, or the person who is the best at not sucking the most.

Life was complicated wherever you went.

Lady Day and Johnny Lennon and Billy Shakes and Bro Van Gogh became his bros and his girl bros, and it was so nice to be accepted and to shine.

He wanted to ask them what it was that he was the best at—for the chip provided no answers to that one question—but it was probably better to play it cool, because maybe that was his greatness, and if he didn't play it cool, he would be kicked off Brogon6969 and there wasn't an earth to go back to.

He also didn't want anyone to tell him that he was the best meathead, in case that was what he was best at, if this planet had a really sick sense of humor, which didn't make a lot of sense.

"We feeling you, bro," Billie and Billy and Johnny and VVG—which sounded a little like vagina, "ta ha ha ha ha ta ha ha ta ta ha"—said to Chad, who also called himself Rad Chad, Bad Chad when he felt sexy and naughty (in a good way), JC, and the C-Note.

"Me too, bros," Chad said. "Me too."

About the Author

Colin Fleming's fiction has appeared in *Commentary*, *VQR*, *Glimmer Train*, *AGNI*, and *Harper's*, with his essays, criticism, and op-eds running in *The Atlantic*, *Rolling Stone*, *Salon*, *The Wall Street Journal*, *The New York Times*, *The Washington Post*, *JazzTimes*, *The New Yorker*, and *The Guardian*. He is a regular guest on many radio programs and podcasts, and is the author of *Buried on the Beaches: Cape Stories for Hooked Hearts and Driftwood Souls*. His website is colinfleminglit.com.

CPSIA information can be obtained
at www.ICGtesting.com
Printed in the USA
BVHW030802091220
595261BV00009B/207